The Legend of
Ranger
The Reindeer Who Couldn't Fly

Alan Salisbury
Illustrated by Roberta Baird

Jabberwocky Books, Minneapolis

Jabberwocky Press
322 First Avenue N, 5th floor
Minneapolis, MN 55401
612.455.2293
www.Jabberwocky-Books.com

ISBN-13: 978-1-62652-333-3
LCCN: 2013948814

Distributed by Itasca Books

Cover Design and Illustrations by Roberta Baird
Typeset by Mary Kristin Ross

Printed in the United States of America

Jabberwocky
Books

All profits from the sale of this book and related Ranger products will be donated to the Antonia J. Giallourakis Endowed Fund in Art Therapy for Children with Cancer at Massachusetts General Hospital.

www.opusonestudios.com

For Ryan, James, Evie, Nikos, and Gabby

Chapter 1

Ranger stood outside Santa's workshop, enjoying the feeling of snowflakes falling on his fur. It was the end of November, and they would not see full sunshine again at the North Pole until March. But the workshop was lit up with a cozy rainbow of twinkling lights. In the distance, the warehouse and the stables where Ranger lived also shone brightly. Santaland was truly a wonderful place to live, especially at this time of year.

Norgrum, the oldest and wisest elf in Santa's workshop, was supervising a crew of elves in loading newly made toys on the sleigh pulled by Ranger to and from the warehouse where they were stored. Ranger waited patiently as the elves crammed rocking horses, skateboards, pogo sticks, dollhouses, and more into the sleigh.

As he was watching the toys being loaded, Ranger heard sleigh bells overhead. He looked up and saw a familiar sight: a team of eight reindeer led by his brother Rudolph, whose famous nose glowed as red as a fire truck, flying through the air. They were practicing for their Christmas Eve flight.

Ranger noticed that Santa himself wasn't in the sleigh, which was being steered by a trusted elf. Ranger guessed Santa was making one of his department store visits to hear what children wanted for Christmas. He liked to do that, so that children would never be sure if they were talking to Santa himself, or to one of his helpers.

Santa's Worksh

Ranger sighed. "That's what I really want to do," he said softly to himself. "Pull Santa's sleigh."

Then he heard a familiar voice say, "You know the rules, Ranger. You have to prove yourself as a flier before you can be hitched to Santa's big sleigh." Ranger turned and saw that his friend Carlanna had come to see him.

Carlanna was the daughter of one of the toymaker elves. She loved all of the reindeer, but Ranger knew he was her favorite. Like the other elf children, she spent most of her day in school. But when school let out, she usually headed right for the workshop or the warehouse to find Ranger. She had made it her job to keep him well groomed. He loved it when she stood on tiptoes to scratch him under the chin.

"You can't fly, can you?" she asked. "Besides, are you sure you want to spend a whole night flying in the middle of winter? Wouldn't you rather be in your warm stable?"

"No, I can't fly," Ranger answered quietly. It was a sore point for him. Not every reindeer could fly, of course, but his own brother could. Why couldn't he? The reindeer that pulled the big sleigh had to be at least three years old, and he'd turned three that summer.

The other reindeer made it look so easy as they got up to speed and just lifted off the ground with the sleigh. But whenever Ranger tried some experimental running starts and athletic leaps on his days off, he always landed right back on the ground. He had tried it so many times, it was embarrassing to him.

Ranger's job was a routine one, but very important. He pulled Santa's utility sleigh to haul the new toys to the warehouse. There they were matched against the wish lists of all the children on Santa's "Nice" list and stored until it was time for the toys to be loaded and delivered on Christmas Eve. His was a full-time job, because the elves in the workshop worked all through the year to make enough toys for all of the world's children.

But Ranger's dream of flying always came to mind as Christmas approached. Now that he was three, Ranger decided that he wanted to see if he could make his dream come true.

"Ready!" called Norgrum. "Off to the warehouse, Ranger!"

"I've made up my mind. I'm going to talk to Norgrum about how I can learn to fly," Ranger said to Carlanna.

"That's a great idea!" she said. "Why not do it today, when you're done with your work?"

So, at the end of a long, hard day hauling toys to the warehouse, Ranger caught up with Norgrum as he was leaving the workshop and worked up the courage to finally ask, "Norgrum, what's the secret of flying?"

Norgrum stopped, stroked his white whiskers, and looked carefully at Ranger. "Why do you ask me that now, Ranger? You've never asked me that before."

"Well," said Ranger, "I love my job, and I know it's important, but my real dream has always been to fly like my brother and the others. I want to be a real part of the team. And besides, I'm three now."

Again, Norgrum paused. "You know, Ranger, not all reindeer can fly. What makes you think that you can fly?"

"I understand that," said Ranger. "But I'm old enough now, and if my brother Rudolph can fly with Santa's sleigh, I think it must be in my blood, too. There has to be a secret to flying that I can learn."

"I see you are growing up, young Ranger," said Norgrum, "and your thinking is on the right track. But if the ability to fly really is in your blood, and if you really are ready to be put to the test, you will figure it out on your own. So I will answer your question this way: The secret lies within!"

"Within? Within what?" asked Ranger.

Norgrum smiled and said, "I will leave it at that. The secret lies within." In a flash, he quickly disappeared around the corner of the workshop and headed toward the office.

Why didn't he just tell me the secret? Ranger thought. *It lies within? Within what?*

As he pondered this, he remembered that he and Norgrum were near the workshop when they were talking. *Maybe he meant that the secret lies within the workshop,* he thought. *But what could it be, and how will I find it?*

Chapter 2

Ranger went inside the workshop. Elves were busy at work on the overtime shift, since Christmas was getting so close. Trying not to disturb the elves, Ranger looked in all the places where the answer might be kept—in drawers, in cupboards, and on shelves all through the workshop. He didn't really know what he was looking for, but he thought the answer might be in an envelope of some kind, or maybe in a special box. He was being as careful as a reindeer could be, as he nosed his way around the workshop and in and out of the closets and storage rooms.

Not finding anything, he decided to ask some of the elves if they could help him discover the secret of flying. Most of the elves just looked at him in a funny way and went on about their business.

Finally, Ranger approached an older elf named Sergland, who was carefully putting the wheels on a shiny red wagon. Ranger knew his name because, like most of the elves in the workshop, Sergland had his name embroidered on the apron he wore over his work clothes.

"What is it, Ranger? Why are you inspecting all of the nooks and crannies of our workshop?" asked Sergland.

"Well," said Ranger, "I've decided that this is the year I want to try to join the flying reindeer team. So I'm working at learning the secret of flying, and I thought the answer might be kept somewhere here in the workshop. Can you help me, Sergland?"

Sergland smiled at him and said, "Have you asked Norgrum?"

"Yes," said Ranger, "but all he would say is: 'The secret lies within.' He wouldn't tell me within what."

"He spoke the truth, Ranger. You must keep searching. The secret does, indeed, lie within," answered the older elf. He turned back to his workbench and picked up the last wheel for the wagon and carefully inspected it.

Well, thought Ranger, I still don't know within what. I guess I'll have to search other places. I'll look in the warehouse, the stables, and maybe even in Santa's house.

The next day, when he had completed his hauling assignments, Ranger decided to search the warehouse, this time with Carlanna helping him.

"What exactly are we looking for?" asked Carlanna. "Didn't Norgrum give you a hint?"

"No, he didn't," responded Ranger. "He said, 'The secret lies within,' and didn't tell me within *what.* So we just have to look in places where someone might keep a special secret."

The warehouse was by far the biggest building in all of Santaland. It had to be very big to store enough toys for all the children in the world.

They opened the big double doors through which Ranger pulled the sleigh many times every day. Inside the warehouse, there were rows and rows of tall shelves overflowing with toys as far as the eye could see. On one side, dolls were in one section, balls in another, scooters in yet another, and so on. And on the other side were just as many rows, but here the toys were grouped by the part of the world they were going to, and then into groups of specific toys that were going to each boy and girl by name.

It was after working hours now, so only two elves were on duty, double-checking the day's work. Next week, the elves would begin round-the-clock shifts to finish the sorting job.

"The warehouse is so big, we can never search it all," Ranger said to Carlanna.

"We don't have to search it all, Ranger," she replied. "We just need to look in the office room and in the closets. The secret wouldn't be mixed in with the toys, I'm sure," she added. So that's what they did.

The results were the same: nothing. And when, just to be sure, Ranger asked one of the elves who was working in the warehouse if he could find the secret of flying there, the elf just looked at him oddly and gave him no answer. Finally he spoke to the gray-haired elf who was the warehouse manager. He, too, would answer only, "The secret, young Ranger, lies within."

*   *   *

At the end of the next day, Ranger and Carlanna went to Santa's house. As they approached the door, Carlanna took hold of Ranger's harness to slow him down.

"You know, Ranger, we can't just search Santa's house. It wouldn't be right," she cautioned.

"I guess you're right, Carlanna," he replied. "But we can ask Mrs. Claus if she knows the secret of flying, or where we can find it."

When she learned what he was searching for, Mrs. Claus would only say, "Bless you, my dear Ranger. I'd like to help you, but you must know that the secret lies within."

Their last stop was the stables. Ranger liked his home here very much. He didn't have his name in fancy lettering on the door to the stall, like the reindeer on Santa's flight crew, or hand-carved troughs for his food and water. But he had a nice, comfortable stall, with soft straw.

Ranger knew pretty much everything about the stables, and there were only a few places where a secret might be hidden there. The search didn't take long. The results were the same as everywhere else: no secret could be found.

As they were leaving the stables, Ranger stopped and said to Carlanna, "Why didn't I think of this before? If anyone can tell me the secret of flying, certainly my own brother will!"

So they turned around and went back inside. Rudolph's stall was the easiest of all to find, because it had a bright-red light bulb lighting up his name above the door. Ranger went directly there. He poked his head over the door and blurted out, "Please, PLEASE, big brother, tell me: What is the secret of flying? I want to be able to fly with Santa, just like you and the others. The only thing anyone will tell me is what Norgrum first told me, that 'the secret lies within.'"

Rudolph looked both surprised and amused as he looked at his younger brother. Silently he thought for a while. Finally he said, "Ranger, my brother, we should have talked about this some time ago. I knew it would come up one day, and now it finally has. As with many surprises here in Santaland, I have always felt that it would be better for you to discover them for yourself rather than for me to just tell you. You are my brother, of course, and I hope you understand that I only want what is best for you.

"As for flying, there is no simple secret I can tell you. The others have all told you the truth. The secret does, indeed, lie within. If you are truly ready to fly, I'm sure you will be able to discover the secret for yourself."

Ranger hesitated, but he thanked Rudolph and headed back to his own stall, disappointed. If even his own brother would not tell him the secret, or *where* to look within, then there was just no way he was going to find it.

Carlanna picked up the currycomb and began to gently brush Ranger. That always made him feel better.

"Maybe next year I will be able to find the secret in time for Christmas," sighed Ranger.

"I'm sure you will find it, Ranger," said Carlanna. "And I will still be here to help you."

So it seemed that Ranger would have to be content with his old job, hauling the new toys from the workshop to the warehouse.

Later that evening, after Carlanna left and Ranger finished his dinner of reindeer chow and freshly melted ice water, he lay down on his sweet-smelling straw for a good night's sleep so he would be rested for another day of toy hauling in the morning. As he was drifting off to the land of Nod, he heard what sounded like coughing from one—no, two—of the reindeer. Then he recognized the gentle voice of Mrs. Claus, who had quietly come into the stables to look after the reindeer. Was that salve he smelled?

"There, there," he thought he heard her say. "This salve medicine should have you feeling better by tomorrow, I'm sure." But her voice sounded concerned.

Finally, Ranger drifted off into a troubled sleep.

Chapter 3

The next morning, Ranger could feel the excitement growing in the stables. Christmas was now only a few days away, and everyone knew they had to work harder than ever to be ready for the big night.

Zarvett, the head reindeer keeper, came to the stables early. Ranger saw him hurry past his stall on his way to talk to one of the flight crew. Then Norgrum entered and went to the same stall. Curious, Ranger got up and followed them to the stall that had Prancer's name above the door. Over the half-door he could see Prancer lying in the straw with his eyes closed and a hot water bottle next to his furry chest.

"I've been checking the team," he heard Zarvett say. "The two we were worried about last night are no better this morning, even after Mrs. Claus rubbed her special salve medicine on their chests. And now two more seem to have this same bug." He shook his head. "I have only seen this kind of illness once before, and that was years ago in the village of Krystalwite, where over a thousand reindeer live. They have a special medicine there that can clear this up within a day. Without that medicine, it could take weeks for our reindeer to recover.

"Oh, noooo," Norgrum moaned. "We need a team of at least *eight* reindeer to keep up with the Christmas Eve schedule and deliver all the toys in one night. On foggy nights, we also need Rudolph. With fewer than six reindeer, a fully loaded sleigh can't get off the ground. Even with seven, it could take two full days to make the trip. It's unheard of for some of the children to *not* get their toys on Christmas morning. The delivery has to happen in one night, or Christmas will be lost!"

Ranger was very troubled when he heard this. "Can I help?" he asked over the stall door.

Norgrum turned and eyed him. "Hmmm, Ranger," he said. "I think perhaps you can. What if I sent Zarvett on a sleigh to Krystalwite to bring back enough medicine for *all* the reindeer, in case even more get sick? I can't risk using any of the Christmas Eve team. They need to save their strength for the big night. But I could use you, Ranger, for this special mission. If you and Zarvett left right away, you would have just enough time to get to Krystalwite, pick up the medicine, and return to the North Pole in time to treat the reindeer.

"That would still give them a day to recover," continued Norgrum. "Yes, that could work, as long as you are back here with the medicine by 5:00 p.m. on December twenty-third. Will you do it, Ranger?" asked Norgrum.

Ranger gulped. "It's scary just thinking about it," he said, "but I know I can do it. I know I *have* to do it, so I *will* do it."

"Then we can't waste any time. Come outside, and Zarvett and I will hitch you up," Norgrum said.

Ranger followed them outside. While Zarvett readied the harness, Norgrum opened the door to the sleigh house next to the stables. Next to the big sleigh that was used only on Christmas Eve was Santa's personal sleigh, which had only two seats. The personal sleigh was just as ornate as the big sleigh and had been lovingly made by the elves with hand-carved scenes from Santaland, and beautiful red-and-green trim.

A young elf appeared, sent by Norgrum, with food and water for both

Ranger and Zarvett. These were quickly loaded into a pack on the sleigh. Just as quickly, Ranger's harness was hitched to the sleigh, and they were ready to go.

"Would you tell Carlanna why I won't see her this afternoon?" he asked the elf, who smiled and nodded.

Within minutes, Ranger and Zarvett were on their way to the village of Krystalwite, a journey of about a day and a half. Ranger had never made such a long trip, but he was excited that he was being entrusted with such an important mission for Santa. *Can I go fast enough?* Ranger asked himself. *I just have to!*

Chapter 4

As they left the gates of Santaland, Ranger looked back at the familiar toy shop, warehouse, and stables, promising himself that they would return in time with the reindeer medicine.

"You won't get to sleep until we reach Krystalwite, you know," Zarvett said, driving the sleigh with a gentle hand on the reins.

"I don't mind," Ranger said, increasing his pace.

The lights of Santaland grew tiny and dim as they made their way toward Krystalwite. At the North Pole in winter, the sun never fully rises, but the sky brightens very late in the morning, and darkens again shortly after noon. Zarvett kept them pointed in the right direction, but Ranger found that he had a good sense of direction and knew which way to go on his own.

Eventually they could see no lights at all in any direction. Only the moonlight reflecting on the snow made it possible to see anything. But there was little to look at anyway– just vast stretches of gleaming white snow, gently rising and falling. Here and there they could see small clumps of trees.

They had been traveling for many hours, and Ranger wondered how soon the dawn would come. Zarvett had dozed off in the sleigh, but Ranger knew the way. Only the soft sound of the runners of the sleigh gliding through the snow could be heard in the otherwise silent night.

It started to snow, gently at first. Ranger thought it was very beautiful.

But as time went on, it snowed harder and harder, and the wind picked up and blew the snow into drifts. With the snow freezing in his beard and hair, Zarvett was awake now and helped to guide Ranger. There was a line of evergreen trees off to the right, and Zarvett directed Ranger toward it.

"Let's stop by the trees for just a few minutes," Zarvett said to Ranger. "We'll get some shelter from the wind, and you can get a quick drink of water and some food."

Zarvett brushed the snow off their cargo pack and found some reindeer treats, which he held out for Ranger. Ranger quickly devoured them, and then suddenly stopped. His ears perked up, and he slowly scanned their surroundings, which were coming back into view as the snow let up some. He focused on the trees right next to them.

Ranger snorted, as reindeer do sometimes to get each other's attention. A second snort was heard, but not from Ranger. A stranger emerged from behind the trees. A caribou was now eyeing them.

Both animals were making strange sounds and moving their heads.

"Can you communicate with him?" asked Zarvett.

"Yes, but not very well," answered Ranger. "And it's a 'her,' not a 'him,'" he added.

"What is she telling you, Ranger?"

"As far as I can make out, she says she's looking to find a safe place amongst the trees," said Ranger. "It's not clear why she wants to find a safe place, but she seems to sense some kind of danger coming. I don't think she really knows what the danger is, but she does seem to be afraid of something."

Zarvett thought about this for some time. "Well, I know animals can often sense danger when humans and elves can't," he said, "but we can't waste any time. We'll leave her a small snack, Ranger. Tell her we wish her well, if you can communicate that to her."

Ranger nodded, and the two animals gestured to each other in their own way.

Quickly they were back on their way. This detour hadn't taken long, so their important journey was still on schedule.

Once again the world was quiet around them. The snow had almost stopped, and they were thankful for that. The moon peeked out now and then as the clouds slowly broke up.

After some time (it was hard to judge the passing of time in the vast open space), the silence was broken by a strange sound. At first it sounded like a distant rumble. *Could it be thunder?* thought Ranger. But now it was getting louder, and Ranger felt the snow and ice shaking beneath his hooves. Then it got so loud that it hurt his ears. The shaking made it almost impossible to pull the sleigh, or even to stand up.

By this time, Zarvett was wide awake. "What's happening, Ranger?" he shouted. It was all he could do to keep from falling out of the sleigh. Then he cried, "Hold on, Ranger, we're having an icequake. Hold *oooonnnnnn!*"

Chapter 5

When the shaking finally stopped, Ranger lay on the ground, still in his harness. The sleigh had tipped on its side, and Zarvett had landed in the snow alongside. *Is Zarvett all right?* worried Ranger. *Am I?* He was scared. He had never experienced anything like what had just happened.

He was relieved to see Zarvett get to his feet, but the look on his face as he brushed off the snow and righted the sleigh didn't make Ranger feel any better. *What was it Zarvett said was happening? An icequake?*

Ranger regained his footing and looked around. They were still surrounded by snow and ice as far as he could see. There were higher drifts in places, and the texture of the snow didn't seem to be as smooth as it had been.

Zarvett walked over to Ranger, and looked him over very slowly and carefully from head to tail. "Are you okay?" he asked, patting Ranger's head. "Yes," said Ranger, "I think so. Just a little shaky. But I think I'm ready to go on."

Zarvett carefully inspected the sleigh to be sure it wasn't damaged. "Everything looks okay," he said. "But we seem to have lost our food and water pack. I don't like the idea of going the rest of the way without it! Wait here, Ranger."

Carefully, Zarvett walked around the area. It was hard to see in the moonlight, with clouds still passing overhead.

"Here it is," said Zarvett. He shook the pack a little and brushed off the remaining snow as he took out two food packets, one for him and one for Ranger.

Then he tucked the pack securely into the back of the sleigh.

"Let's eat before we go on," Zarvett said. "I hope we can make Krystalwite by tonight, Ranger."

As quickly as they could, they had a small meal and a drink and were back on their journey.

*   *   *

It was hours later. The sun had risen and set not long after they had eaten. That was a long time ago, and the moonlight once again made the snow and ice glisten softly. Ranger was tired and did his best to keep a steady pace.

On the horizon, they saw the first glimmer of lights. Krystalwite! "We're getting close," Zarvett said to encourage Ranger. Soon, they were approaching the gates of Krystalwite.

Like Santaland, Krystalwite was hundreds of years old. It was the original home of the colony of elves that lived in the region. Many of the elf families that now called Santaland their home had come from Krystalwite long, long ago. It was a much bigger village than Santaland. Most of the buildings had steep roofs and beautiful trim around the windows and doors and under the eaves. The elves of Krystalwite were skilled craftsmen and craftswomen, like those in Santaland.

As they passed through the gates, Zarvett directed Ranger to the home of his friend Arjenna, who lived over the Krystalwite Reindeer Clinic.

A big smile came over Arjenna's face as she opened the door. "Zarvett, my dear friend, it's been far too long since we have seen one another," she said as they embraced warmly. "What brings you all the way to Krystalwite so close to Christmas?"

Zarvett thanked Arjenna and quickly explained his mission. "As you know,

my dear friend, the medicine will take nearly a full day to work its cure and allow Santa's team to recover for their trip," Zarvett said. "So we have little time to lose. Ranger, the reindeer who brought me here, will eat and rest up while we load the sleigh with your medicine."

Ranger, who was nearly falling asleep on his feet, perked up at the thought of food and rest.

"Of course, Zarvett. I understand completely. But there is one small problem. We haven't had much of this sickness here in the last few years, and I only have two doses of that medicine on hand. So we will have to prepare more. I'm afraid that will take several hours," said Arjenna. "From what you tell me, that will get you back to the workshop many hours later than you planned."

"Then we must get started making the additional medicine immediately, Arjenna," responded Zarvett. "We'll have to make up the time on the return trip somehow, or Christmas may be lost!"

Ranger prepared as best he could for a fast trip home. He enjoyed a good dinner and napped in the warm stall that Arjenna led him to. He wanted to be all ready when they completed loading the medicine in the sleigh. But he had used every ounce of energy he could muster to get here as fast as he could. How could he go even faster on the way home?

Chapter 6

---

*I*t was around midnight on the evening of December 22 when Zarvett gently shook Ranger awake. "We're ready!" he said. "We have enough doses to make all the reindeer on our Christmas team healthy!" The elves who worked in Arjenna's clinic quickly loaded the medicine on the sleigh, harnessed Ranger, and said their goodbyes. Zarvett and Ranger were off on their return trip.

"Goodbye, dear friends, and good luck," called Arjenna as the sleigh pulled away and headed for the gates of Krystalwite. "The children of the world are counting on you!"

But they had to be back at Santa's stables by 5:00 p.m. How could they make a day-and-a-half trip in less than a day? Ranger picked up his pace and followed the tracks he had made on the way to Krystalwite, so it was easier to stay on course.

They were soon out of sight of the village lights, and Ranger was happy to have the moonlight to help him find the way. Still, he didn't see how they could get back to Santaland in time to give the reindeer their medicine and let it do its work.

Hours went by and, as before, there was little to see except for the gently rolling snow and ice as they continued following their original tracks. They had passed by the place where they'd been when the icequake struck. Ranger could feel his muscles begin to ache as he fought off tiredness.

There were no clouds in the sky now. In the bright moonlight, Ranger could see that something on the horizon looked different, but he was not sure why.

Determined not to let himself feel tired, he galloped on, looking anxiously ahead.

Now he was sure there was something in their path ahead, but he couldn't tell what it was. A dark line was getting bigger and bigger as they approached it.

Zarvett was concerned, too. "Slow down, Ranger, until we're sure it's safe to keep going," he said.

Finally it became clear what lay ahead. There was an opening in the snow and ice cover in front of them, and the closer they got to it, the bigger it seemed to be. Ranger slowed down to a walk and approached carefully.

He could hardly believe what he saw. There was a huge gap in the ice that must have been at least fifty feet across.

As he peered carefully over the edge, he couldn't see the bottom. And the opening extended as far as he could see to his left and right.

"What happened?" Ranger asked Zarvett. "Did we take a wrong turn?" But that was impossible, because he'd been following his own tracks across the snow.

Zarvett shook his head. "It's called a crevasse, Ranger, a very large and deep crack in the ice, and it was caused by the icequake we felt on our way to Krystalwite. Now we just have to get to the other side." He tried to sound cheerful, but Ranger could tell from his voice that all hope of getting the medicine to the stables in time was now lost.

Chapter 7

"*I* can get us across," said Ranger suddenly.

"You can what?" answered Zarvett.

"I said I can get us across," repeated Ranger.

"And how do you think you will do that, Ranger?" asked Zarvett.

"I'm not really sure how, but I just know that if I try hard enough, I can do it. I feel it deep within myself, and I'm not afraid," countered Ranger.

As he said the words "within myself," Ranger suddenly thought of what Norgrum and the others had all said to him: "The secret lies within." *That must be it*, thought Ranger. *The secret is not within something, it's within me! Maybe I can fly after all!*

Zarvett thought it over. Finally he told Ranger, "Well, if we don't try to cross the crevasse, we most certainly will fail in our mission. It's better to try and not succeed than to fail without even trying."

They turned the sleigh around and went backward several hundred feet, to give Ranger a running start. They turned around once again and faced the crevasse.

"I'm ready when you are," said Zarvett. "Take your time."

Ranger looked at what lay ahead of them. He saw the edge of the crevasse on the near side, but focused his eyes on the goal: the far side he had to reach. He knew that was much farther than he or any other reindeer could jump, even with a running start. But he also knew that there was no other choice.

"If you find that you can't . . . that you don't . . . take off," said Zarvett, "there might still be time to stop." Ranger shook his head. He could not try to fly thinking he might fail.

Taking a deep breath and keeping his eyes firmly fixed on the other side of the crevasse, he started forward, slowly at first. Then he picked up speed, running faster and faster until he was pulling the sleigh as fast as he possibly could. As they approached the edge, he thought once again of Norgrum's words, dug in his hooves, and pushed off the ice as hard as he could.

Ranger felt himself and the sleigh lifting off and climbing. This was unlike any of his many earlier failed attempts at flying. The rush of air in his face was wonderful. He could not believe the excitement that swept over him.

But wait! He suddenly realized that they were starting to fall back down. Was he going to fail once again when so much was at stake?

Ranger could still see the far side, and he felt a new wave of energy as he put all thoughts of failure out of his head.

"I can *do* this, I can *do* this!" he said over and over to himself. "I *have* to fly to save Christmas!" He kicked and kicked as hard as he could with all four legs, again and again, pulling his way through the cold air under the night sky.

But were they still falling?

Chapter 8

---

*I*f anyone had been able to look down from the sky overhead at the scene below, they would have seen the large crevasse, of course, and the beautiful glimmer of the moonlight on the snow and ice on either side. They would have seen the double set of tracks from the sleigh runners and the reindeer's hooves, leading up to the edge on the side in the direction of Krystalwite, but only a single set of tracks on the other side. Looking down into the crevasse, they would have been able to see many small chunks of snow and ice that had fallen from the edge where the sleigh took off. But they would not have seen any sign of the sleigh, its passenger, or a reindeer. The sleigh with Zarvett on board and Ranger in the lead had not fallen into the crevasse, but had flown out of sight . . . and they would fly all the way back to Santaland at the North Pole! Not only would they make up the lost time, but they would arrive hours ahead of schedule, thanks to their speed.

Soon Ranger, Zarvett, and the sleigh were circling over Santaland, and just as quickly they were landing on the snow-covered ice. Elves appeared from every building, clapping and cheering.

Zarvett lost no time unloading the medicine and taking it to the stables to begin treating the reindeer.

Carlanna arrived, laughing and crying at the same time, and gave Ranger the biggest hug ever. "I knew you could do it, Ranger," she yelled.

Norgrum beamed with pride as he unhooked Ranger from the sleigh. He,

too, gave him a big hug. "I see that you have made a great discovery, Ranger. And you made it on your own. You believed in yourself and realized your dream. Congratulations!"

"Thank you, Norgrum," said Ranger. "And thank you for believing in me. Now, if you don't mind, I really need to eat something and get some sleep!" He tried to hide a yawn, which is not easy for a reindeer to do.

"You've earned that, Ranger, and then some," responded Norgrum. "When you are rested up, I want to hear all about your trip. I'm sure it was quite an adventure."

Santa himself came out the door of the workshop. "I have heard great things about you, young Ranger, and your brother is bursting with pride about your accomplishment.

"I am indebted to you," continued Santa. "Indeed, the world's children are indebted to you. There is no doubt about it, you have saved Christmas! You are now a full-fledged member of Santa's Christmas Eve reindeer team."

This was what Ranger had waited all his life to hear. Santa's words echoed in his mind as he ate a good meal and fell happily to sleep in his stall.

He continued to haul toys to the warehouse, because he loved his job. But whenever Santa needed him on Christmas Eve, Ranger was ready to join the team and fly through the air on the most magical night of the year!